NO MONKEYS IN THE PARK

A sequel to *No Monkeys in the Library*

Today is a nice, sunny day and Bungle, the monkey, is sitting in his library reading a book.

Bungle finishes the last book in his library. Now, he needs a new book to read.

So, Bungle decides to go to the library to get a new book.

On the way to the library,
he notices a park.

He watches people swing on swings, kids slide down slides, families walk on trails, and ducks...do whatever ducks do.

Bungle decides to go to the park instead.

At the park, Bungle approaches some ducks swimming in the pond.

Bungle thinks the ducks
look hungry.

So, Bungle feeds the ducks.

"No feeding the ducks!" the park ranger yells.

"NO MONKEYS IN THE PARK!"

The ducks are having fun
swimming in the pond.
Bungle wants to have
fun, too.

So, Bungle swims with the ducks.

"No swimming in the pond!" the park ranger shouts.

"NO MONKEYS IN THE PARK!"

Bungle walks out of the pond and is very wet.

Bungle uses a picnic
blanket to dry off.

"No stealing picnic blankets!" the park ranger barks.

"NO MONKEYS IN THE PARK!"

Bungle listens to his belly growl and realizes he's hungry.

Bungle spots an apple tree but he can't reach the apples.

So, he climbs the tree.

"No climbing the apple trees!" the park ranger hollers.

"NO MONKEYS IN THE PARK!"

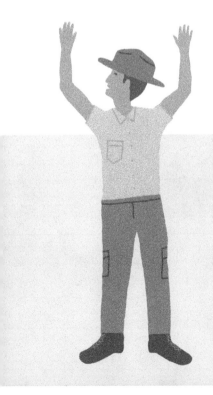

Bungle decides he wants to go down a slide.

He doesn't see the ladder,
so he climbs up the slide.

"No climbing up the slide!"
the park ranger bellows.

"NO MONKEYS
IN THE PARK!"

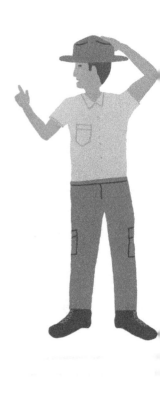

Bungle overhears a family
talking about feeding
the ducks.

Bungle tells them that they shouldn't feed the ducks.

As Bungle leaves the pond, he trips on a piece of trash.

Bungle notices a trash can. Bungle decides to throw away the trash.

"Good job helping out around the park!" the park ranger says kindly. "I think you would be a perfect..."

"...junior ranger!"

Paige Mulder was born in Michigan. She has two younger brothers and a younger sister, Luke, Ben, and Megan. Paige started her writing career at 13 years old. Her first book, *No Monkeys in the Library*, was originally a 7th grade homework assignment. Paige enjoyed writing the book so much that she decided to self-publish it and continue to write more books.

Find more information about Paige and her books at paigemulder.com

Other Books by Paige Mulder

No Monkeys in the Library

Alonso the Space Dinosaur

**Coming Soon
July 20, 2021**

9 781736 673706